SHAKESPEARE FOR EVERYONE

RICHARD III

By Jennifer Mulherin and Abigail Frost
Illustrations by Gwen Green
CHERRYTREE BOOKS

Author's note

There is no substitute for seeing the plays of Shakespeare performed. Only then can you really understand why Shakespeare is our greatest dramatist and poet. This book simply gives you the background to the play and tells you about the story and characters. It will, I hope, encourage you to see the play.

A Cherrytree Book

Designed and produced by
A S Publishing

Published in 2006 by Cherrytree Press,
a division of the Evans Publishing Group,
2A Portman Mansions, Chiltern St, London WIU 6NR

Reprinted 2006

British Library Cataloguing in Publication Data
Mulherin, Jennifer
   Richard III
    1. Drama in English. Shakespeare, William, 1564-1616
    I. Title II. Series III Frost, Abigail.
    822.3'3

ISBN 1 84234 049 2
13-digit ISBN 978 1 84234 049 3

Printed in China through Colorcraft Ltd., Hong Kong

Contents

Richard III *and Shakespeare's history*

RICARDVS · III · ANG · REX ·

Richard III by an unknown artist. During Tudor times, the king's portrait was altered to make him look grotesque.

King Richard III was born in 1452, and died at Bosworth Field in 1485. Although he reigned for only just over two years, he is one of the most famous (or infamous) kings in British history. Shakespeare's play is undoubtedly a large part of the reason.

Richard III is one of Shakespeare's ten *history plays*. All but two of them tell a continuous story, from Richard II's reign until the start of Henry VII's, though they were not written in chronological order.

Shakespeare was the first to write history plays of this kind, and they were very popular. With their pageantry and exciting battle scenes, they had the same appeal as today's epic films.

York and Lancaster

The plays show how the descendants of King Edward III fought for the throne, dividing into the 'Houses' of York and Lancaster. In *Richard II*, the Lancastrian Henry Bolingbroke seizes the throne from his cousin, the weak young King Richard, who is killed in Pontefract Castle. Bolingbroke becomes King Henry IV. There are two plays about his reign *(Henry IV Parts 1 and 2)*. He reigns well, but dies tormented by guilt about Richard's death. The plays show his wars against Northern rebels, and how his son, Prince Hal, gives up an idle, drunken life to fight and show himself fit to be king in turn. One of his drinking-companions is the fat knight Sir John Falstaff, Shakespeare's greatest comic character.

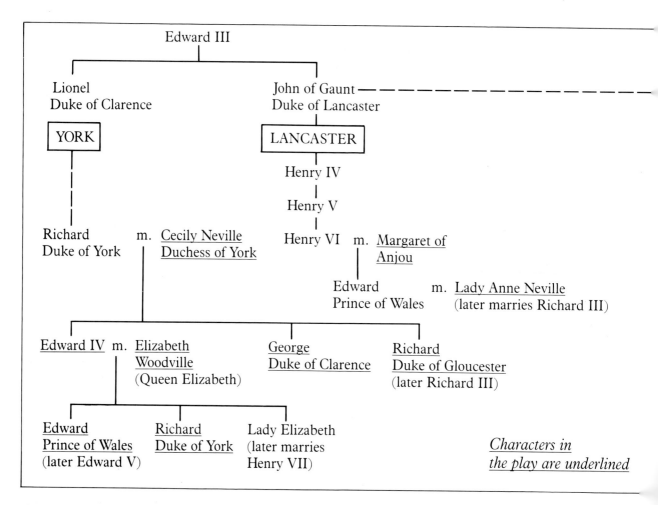

Edward III

Lionel
Duke of Clarence

John of Gaunt — — — — — — — — — — — — —
Duke of Lancaster

YORK

LANCASTER

Henry IV

Henry V

Richard
Duke of York

m. <u>Cecily Neville</u>
<u>Duchess of York</u>

Henry VI m. <u>Margaret of</u>
<u>Anjou</u>

Edward   m. <u>Lady Anne Neville</u>
Prince of Wales   (later marries Richard III)

<u>Edward IV</u> m. <u>Elizabeth</u>
<u>Woodville</u>
(Queen Elizabeth)

<u>George</u>
<u>Duke of Clarence</u>

<u>Richard</u>
<u>Duke of Gloucester</u>
(later Richard III)

<u>Edward</u>
<u>Prince of Wales</u>
(later Edward V)

<u>Richard</u>
<u>Duke of York</u>

Lady Elizabeth
(later marries
Henry VII)

Characters in
the play are underlined

A simplified family tree
showing the houses of
Lancaster and York at the
time of Richard III.
Henry VII, who ruled
after Richard, was the
first monarch of the House
of Tudor.

Margaret m. Edmund Tudor
Beaufort | Earl of Richmond

| TUDOR |

Henry
Earl of Richmond
(later Henry VII)

In *Henry V*, Prince Hal, now king, inspires his army to win lands in France for England. He makes peace with the French and marries a French princess, Katherine. But he dies when his son, another Henry, is a baby – and all that he has gained is lost.

Wars of the Roses

Henry VI is in three parts. In the first, the lords who rule England while the king is a child struggle among themselves, and the French, led by Joan of Arc, win back the lands the English held. As part of the peace settlement, the boy Henry is married to Princess Margaret of Anjou (who appears in

A fanciful nineteenth-century painting showing hostile lords, in the Temple Gardens, picking red and white roses in support of their 'sides' in the Wars of the Roses.

Richard and Lady Anne dressed in their coronation robes. There is no evidence that Richard poisoned his wife, though he was disappointed that she had only one son – who died before her.

Richard III as a bitter old woman). Parts 2 and 3 show how England became torn by civil war, the Wars of the Roses. In a scene in the Temple Gardens, London, lords choose roses to show their support, red for Lancaster or white for York. Richard Plantagenet, son of the disgraced Duke of York, leads the Yorkists. His sons, Edward Earl of March and Richard Duke of Gloucester, work to win the throne, both in open battle and by killing off those who oppose them behind the scenes.

Henry has grown up to be a pious man, often too occupied with religious matters to protect himself. His wife Margaret makes up for him, leading his troops into battle. But at last Henry is captured and deposed. Edward is crowned king, but the Lancastrians fight back. At the battle of Tewkesbury Henry's son is killed; Margaret is banished and the Lancastrians are finished. But Henry, a prisoner in the Tower of London, is still a threat to the Yorkists. Richard and Edward kill him. The stage is now set for the play of *Richard III*.

Shakespeare's sources
Shakespeare got his facts from chroniclers of his own time, especially Raphael Holinshed and Edward Hall. Hall's account of Richard III's life is based on one by Sir Thomas More, Henry VIII's friend and adviser who was executed when he would not support Henry's plan to divorce his first wife. As a boy, More lived in the household of John Morton, the Bishop of Ely in *Richard III*. As a member of Richard's council, Morton had access to 'inside information'. When Richard sends Ely away to fetch strawberries, this might well be a real incident which the bishop told More years later.

But More, then Henry VIII's trusted friend, was of course on the side of the Tudors: the Earl of Richmond in the play (later Henry VII), was the king's father. Elizabeth, Henry

VIII's daughter, was queen in Shakespeare's day, and naturally Tudor historians assumed that Richmond was in the right when he seized the throne. This has led some critics to dismiss Shakespeare's plays as pure propaganda for the Tudors.

Drama before history

But Shakespeare was more interested in creating a fast-moving drama than in propaganda. The play seems to cover a much shorter time than the events in it really took. For example, after seeing his brother Clarence led to the Tower of London, Richard goes straight to Henry VI's funeral, where he courts Lady Anne; but in fact the funeral took place seven years before Clarence was imprisoned, and Richard married Anne between the two events. By telescoping time in this way, Shakespeare focuses attention on Richard's ruthlessness.

Even further from the facts is old Queen Margaret's part in the play. In 'real life' she was banished to France in 1476, and died in 1482, nearly a year before Richard took the throne. Shakespeare's audience would remember her as a strong character in the three *Henry VI* plays, and by her angry curses on Richard and Edward she reminds us how they usurped Henry's throne.

Shakespeare also makes Richard much more of a villain than even the most prejudiced of the Tudor chroniclers depicted him. Right from the start he shows Richard 'determined to prove a villain'.

Just like modern television audiences, Elizabethan play-goers liked to see a really 'good' villain. Their idea of what made a villain was partly based on a distorted view of the Italian political writer, Niccolo Machiavelli (1469-1527). In his book *The Prince*, he advised rulers to be cunning and ruthless in their quest to win and keep power. English

A romantic scene from the battle field. Under the approving eye of his horse, Henry Tudor picks dead Richard's crown from amongst the bushes on Bosworth Field.

dramatists portrayed 'machiavels' – villains who wilfully ignore morality, religion and human kindness to get their way. Richard is a villain of this kind; so are Iago (in *Othello*) and Edmund (in *King Lear*).

Shakespeare emphasised Richard's wickedness by drawing attention to his deformed body. He had a hunched back

Richard's well-thumbed prayer book must have been in regular use.

and a withered arm, although neither is very noticeable in early portraits of him. (Some were altered in the Tudor period to make him look worse.) The Elizabethans were willing to accept that, on stage at least, a person's appearance reflected their nature.

But Shakespeare's Richard III also has a great deal of charm. Some of his enemies, for example Queen Elizabeth and Queen Margaret, are as ruthless as he is. He deceives people by skilful acting, and he has a grim sense of humour. As the play proceeds, the audience may sympathise with him against their will.

Who killed the princes?

Some people today think Richard has been misjudged – especially over the deaths of young Edward V and his brother. They suggest that the boys may have been killed by someone else wishing to please Richard, or even that they may have outlived him and been killed by Henry VII.

It is very unlikely that any real, new evidence for either side will appear. The bones of two children were found buried under a staircase in the Tower in the time of King Charles II, and reburied in Westminster Abbey. They are probably the princes' (what other children would be buried there?), but they obviously cannot reveal who gave the order to kill them.

Richard's heraldic symbol was a wild boar, a fierce and tenacious animal.

Where are the princes?

Richard's supporters point to the fact that he was a religious man; his well-used prayer book, complete with a long prayer he wrote himself, still exists. But he was a medieval king, whose claim to the throne was very shaky as long as the princes lived; and kings in the Middle Ages often had those who stood in their way killed. When the princes ceased to appear in the Tower gardens, the rumour soon spread that they were dead, and many people grew very angry. In fact, public outrage may have lost Richard the Battle of Bosworth – some of his former supporters joined Richmond's forces, as we see in the play.

Richard was not the last English monarch to dispose of his enemies; the Tudors did so too. But they at least tried their enemies publicly for treason before they were executed. The princes' fate was more horrific, to people of Richard's time as well as Shakespeare's and ours, because they were condemned and killed in secret.

The Princes in the Tower *by Millais. If the boys were alive, why did Richard not stop rumours that he had killed them by showing them in public?*

The story of King Richard III

England is at peace at last after years of civil war. King Edward IV is secure on the throne he seized from Henry VI; his mind is now on love, not war. But his brother, the hunchbacked Richard, Duke of Gloucester, finds no pleasure in this new mood. He, 'determined to prove a villain', is plotting to gain power.

Peace and bitterness
Now is the winter of our discontent
Made glorious summer by this sun of York;
And all the clouds that lour'd upon our house
In the deep bosom of the ocean buried.
                                          . . .

I, that am rudely stamp'd, and want love's majesty
To strut before a wanton ambling nymph;
                                          . . .

Why, I, in this weak piping time of peace,
Have no delight to pass away the time,
Unless to see my shadow in the sun
And descant on mine own deformity:

                                          Act I Sc i

Richard's plots are bearing fruit already. He meets his brother George, Duke of Clarence, bound for the Tower of London, under arrest. A prophecy says that the king's sons will be killed by a usurper whose initial is 'G'; the king suspects Clarence. Richard suggests the queen's family, the Woodvilles, are to blame. No man is safe from their malice: even Lord Hastings, the Lord Chamberlain, had to beg the queen to be freed from the Tower.

Sir Robert Brackenbury, the Lieutenant of the Tower, interrupts. The brothers pretend to be exchanging Court gossip. Clarence is led away to prison, not realising it was Richard who spread the tale that condemned him. The Duke of Gloucester wants his brother dead.

Lord Hastings, just released from the Tower, stops and says the king is ill. This is bad news for Richard. It will upset his plans if Edward dies before Clarence.

A strange courtship

Richard plans to marry Lady Anne, daughter of Warwick, the powerful 'kingmaker', and widow of King Henry VI's son, Edward, whom Richard killed. Richard watches her sadly following the coffin of another of his victims – Henry VI, who died mysteriously in the Tower. She curses Henry's killer, and his future wife and child as well.

Anne's curse
O! cursed be the hand that made these holes;
Cursed the heart that had the heart to do it!
Cursed the blood that let this blood from hence!
More direful hap betide that hated wretch,
That makes us wretched by the death of thee,
Than I can wish to adders, spiders, toads,
Or any creeping venom'd thing that lives!

Act I Sc ii

Richard tells the coffin-bearers to stop while he talks to Anne, who calls him a 'minister of Hell'. Henry's wounds, she says, are bleeding again in his killer's presence. Richard asks to put his side of the story. Anne refuses, but he persists, saying he did not kill her husband – his brother, King Edward, did. He admits killing Henry, but says the saintly

king was fitter for Heaven than Earth. Somehow, he always has an excuse, and the next is the most daring of all. He says that Anne is to blame for his victims' deaths – he would kill

Confession
Nay, do not pause; for I did kill King Henry;
But 'twas thy beauty that provoked me.
Nay, now dispatch; 'twas I that stabb'd young Edward;
But 'twas thy heavenly face that set me on.
Take up the sword again, or take up me.

Act I Sc ii

everyone in the world if it would help him to marry her. Anne spits at him, but he still pleads his love. At last he offers her his sword, to kill him if she wishes.

As she moves to stab him, he confesses that he did kill her husband. Anne's feelings towards him change. Thinking he has repented, she accepts his ring. He asks her to wait while he escorts Henry's body to his grave.

Richard exults in his own audacity. 'Was ever woman in this humour wooed? Was ever woman in this humour won?'

13

The queen's fears

At the palace, Queen Elizabeth is anxious about her husband. Will he live? If he dies, her young son Edward will be king – and Richard, whom she hates, will rule as Lord Protector until he is grown up. The Duke of Buckingham and Lord Stanley bring news from the king's bedside. He wants to make peace between the Woodvilles and Richard's side. Next Richard himself comes in, with Lord Hastings. He complains that the Woodvilles are making trouble by flattering the king, while he, a 'plain man' who cannot behave that way, is made out to be a traitor. The queen says that Richard is envious; he accuses her of having Clarence and Hastings imprisoned.

Queen Margaret's curse

Elizabeth threatens to tell the king what Richard has said. While they argue, old Queen Margaret, Henry VI's widow, who hates them all, slips in. Though banished, she cannot resist seeing her enemies. At last she speaks up – saying she should be queen. She curses Elizabeth, who took her place as queen; the courtiers, who helped Edward overthrow her husband; and most of all Richard – may he die at the height of his sins! She warns Buckingham that Richard will be his death.

A warning

O Buckingham! take heed of yonder dog:
Look, when he fawns, he bites; and when he bites
His venom tooth will rankle to the death:
Have not to do with him, beware of him;
Sin, death and hell have set their marks on him,
And all their ministers attend on him.

Act I Sc iii

Richard says he cannot blame the old queen for her anger. But his good, Christian piety is a sham. His next act is to pass on an order from the king – Clarence's death-warrant.

Clarence's end

In his room at the Tower, Clarence goes to sleep again, after a night of bad dreams – dreams of drowning. Two hired murderers enter the room. One has stirrings of conscience, but thinks of the reward. Clarence wakes; realising why they have come, he appeals to their consciences. They say they

---

Clarence's dream

Lord, Lord! methought what pain it was to drown:
What dreadful noise of water in mine ears!
What sights of ugly death within mine eyes!
Methought I saw a thousand fearful wracks;
A thousand men that fishes gnaw'd upon;
Wedges of gold, great anchors, heaps of pearl,
Inestimable stones, unvalu'd jewels,
All scatter'd in the bottom of the sea.
Some lay in dead men's skulls; and in those holes
Where eyes did once inhabit, there were crept,
As 'twere in scorn of eyes, reflecting gems,
That woo'd the slimy bottom of the deep,
And mock'd the dead bones that lay scatter'd by.

Act I Sc iv

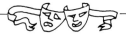

have come on the king's orders. He says Richard will reward them if they spare him, but they laugh. He even says they can save their souls by mercy, but they attack him, then drown him in a barrel of his favourite Malmsey wine. Now, too late, the second murderer repents.

15

Edward's repentance

Knowing he is dying, the king wants to leave his friends at peace among themselves. He makes them all embrace each other. But one person is missing – Clarence. The queen asks Edward to free him. Richard pretends to take offence, saying everyone knows Clarence is dead. Edward says he ordered him to be reprieved. Richard says it was too late – the messenger was a 'tardy cripple'. He means himself. Edward bitterly regrets Clarence's death.

Richard starts to spread the word that the Woodvilles were to blame. Even Clarence's own children believe this slur; Richard was kind to them. But their grandmother, the old Duchess of York, knows his true nature. Queen Elizabeth enters in great distress. The king is dead. The duchess has now lost two sons.

A cracked mirror
I have bewept a worthy husband's death,
And liv'd with looking on his images;
But now two mirrors of his princely semblance
Are crack'd in pieces by malignant death,
And I for comfort have but one false glass,
That grieves me when I see my shame in him.

Act II Sc ii

Richard comes to beg his mother's blessing. She asks God to make him kind and virtuous. Talk turns to Prince Edward – the heir to the throne. He will travel to London with only a few men to guard him, since the country is at peace. Richard plans to capture him from the Woodvilles.

As Queen Elizabeth sits with her younger son the Duke of York, she hears Richard has captured her supporters Rivers, Grey and Vaughan, who were in charge of Prince Edward.

She flees to the sanctuary of Westminster Abbey, where church law will protect her from imprisonment.

The boy king

Richard escorts his nephew Prince Edward into London. The prince says he wants more uncles – the queen's brothers – to greet him, but Richard says they are his enemies.

Prince Edward asks where he is to stay until he is crowned. Richard suggests the Tower. The Prince does not like the idea – Henry VI and Clarence both died there – but accepts it. His brother York arrives. When he hears they are going to the Tower, York is afraid of Clarence's ghost. The prince says he is not afraid of dead uncles. Richard hopes he is not afraid of live ones. The boys exchange jokes about Richard's hunched back. As the boys leave, Buckingham wonders if Elizabeth has told York to insult Richard.

Now Richard and his friends make plans. They will hold two councils – one to arrange the coronation, one to make sure it does not take place. They must find out which side Lord Hastings is on; if he insists on Edward being crowned, they must chop off his head. They send Sir William Catesby to speak to him.

False confidence

Hastings learns that his friend Lord Stanley is worried; he has dreamed that the boar, Richard's emblem, has removed his helmet, leaving him unprotected. He is also suspicious of the idea of holding two councils (how will they know what is decided at the other one?), and suggests fleeing while there is time. Hastings thinks they are safe, because their friend Catesby will keep them informed. But Catesby is in Richard's power.

The roots of war

At Pontefract Castle in the north of England, Rivers, Grey and Vaughan are executed. Years before, Henry VI's grandfather Henry IV had King Richard II murdered there. This

act meant his family, the House of Lancaster, was doomed to lose the throne in civil war.

Hastings and the rest of the council meet to discuss the coronation. Richard enters and stops the discussion by asking the Bishop of Ely to send for some strawberries from his garden. Then he and Buckingham leave the room, certain that Hastings will not agree to their plans.

Returning with the strawberries, the bishop asks after Richard. Hastings says he was in good spirits. But Richard's mood is changed on his return. He accuses Queen Elizabeth of conspiring to bewitch him, showing his withered arm (which he was born with) as proof. Hastings starts to defend Elizabeth; Richard uses this excuse to have him arrested. He goes off to the block.

A curse fulfilled
Now Margaret's curse is fall'n upon our heads,
When she exclaim'd on Hastings, you, and I,
For standing by when Richard stabb'd her son.

Act III Sc iii

Woe for England
Woe, woe, for England! not a whit for me;
For I, too fond, might have prevented this.
Stanley did dream the boar did raze his helm;
And I did scorn it, and distain'd to fly.
Three times to-day my foot-cloth horse did stumble,
And startled when he looked upon the Tower,
As loath to bear me to the slaughter-house.

. . .

O Margaret, Margaret! now thy heavy curse
Is lighted on poor Hastings' wretched head.

Act III Sc iv

Slander

Once Hastings is beheaded, Richard is free to blacken his rival's name. He says Prince Edward and his young brother York are bastards – Edward IV was legally married to someone else when he married Elizabeth. The king was also a tyrant; he killed a man for calling his son heir to the 'crown', meaning a house of that name. Richard tells Buckingham to spread these slurs among the citizens of London, then bring the Lord Mayor to his house.

But Buckingham does not find this easy. Unable to make a citizens' meeting acclaim Richard as king, he has to get his own men to hide at the back and cry 'God save King Richard!' But he persuades the Lord Mayor to come.

When Catesby announces the mayor's arrival, Richard pretends to be busy praying with two priests. But he is 'persuaded' to come out, and asks the mayor if he has done something to offend the citizens. Buckingham says his offence is to have allowed Edward the throne, when he himself is rightful heir. Richard responds with false modesty; Buckingham repeats the charges against Prince

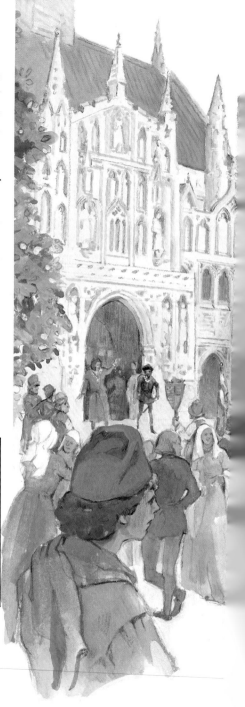

Hypocrisy

Cousin of Buckingham, and sage, grave men,
Since you will buckle fortune on my back,
To bear her burden, whe'r I will or no,
I must have patience to endure the load:
For God doth know, and you may partly see,
How far I am from the desire of this.

Act III Sc vii

Edward. Richard keeps refusing, until his visitors leave – but Catesby makes him call them back. This time Richard accepts the offer – 'against my conscience and my soul'.

'Long live Richard, England's worthy king!' cries Buckingham. Richard returns to his prayers.

Summons to Westminster

Three royal ladies meet by the Tower: Anne, Elizabeth and the old Duchess of York. They have all come to visit the princes; Anne has brought Clarence's daughter to meet her cousins. But Brackenbury turns them away on the king's orders. 'The king? Who's that?' asks Elizabeth. 'I mean the Lord Protector,' says Brackenbury, hastily. They learn the truth when Lord Stanley arrives to take Anne to be crowned queen at Westminster Abbey.

Elizabeth is devastated to hear Richard has taken the throne. Remembering Queen Margaret's curse, she warns her son, the Marquis of Dorset, to flee abroad; he can join Henry, Earl of Richmond, who is gathering an army in France. The duchess, too, is upset by the news; her own son has usurped her grandson's throne! Even Anne is in distress; remembering how she cursed his wife – herself – she fears that Richard will kill her. Departing, Elizabeth takes a last look at the Tower, where her sons are in great peril.

The prisoners
Stay yet, look back with me unto the Tower.
Pity, you ancient stones, those tender babes
Whom envy hath immur'd within your walls,
Rough cradle for such little pretty ones!
Rude ragged nurse, old sullen playfellow
For tender princes, use my babies well.
So foolish sorrow bids your stones farewell.

Act IV Sc i

21

A king afraid

Richard sits on the throne in Westminster Abbey, newly-crowned, but still not safe. He drops a dark hint to Buckingham – is he really king while Prince Edward lives? Buckingham will not rise to the bait, so Richard has to make himself plain: the princes must be killed, quickly. Buckingham says he will consider it. Angrily, Richard asks a page to find him a man who will kill for money. He decides not to trust Buckingham any more.

Lord Stanley brings the news that Elizabeth's son Dorset has gone to join Richmond. Richard's foes are gathering fast. It is time for him to get a new wife – Edward's daughter Elizabeth, who will be heir to the throne when her brothers are dead. He tells Catesby to spread a rumour that Anne is very ill. Sir James Tyrrell arrives – the man willing to kill the princes. Richard whispers his orders and he leaves on his dreadful mission.

Now that Richard is king, Buckingham wants some lands he was promised. But Richard has already turned against him, and his mind is on other things. He remembers that Stanley's wife is the Earl of Richmond's mother; is she an enemy at court? Now he remembers how Henry VI met Richmond as a boy, and prophesied he would be king; and an Irish bard prophesied that Richard would die when he saw Richmond. Buckingham has chosen the wrong moment for his plea. Richard brushes him off. Insulted, and afraid, Buckingham decides to leave Richard's side.

Murderers' tears

Tyrrell has murdered the princes in the Tower; but he is shaken by the experience. He has left the two hardened villains he took to help him in tears at the horror of killing children. Richard questions him. Is he sure the boys are dead? Are they safely buried?

> **Marriage of convenience**
> *I must be married to my brother's daughter,*
> *Or else my kingdom stands on brittle glass.*
> *Murder her brothers, and then marry her!*
> *Uncertain way of gain! But I am in*
> *So far in blood, that sin will pluck on sin:*
> *Tear-falling pity dwells not in this eye.*
>
> Act IV Sc ii

Innocent blood

The tyrannous and bloody act is done;
The most arch deed of piteous massacre
That ever yet this land was guilty of.

        . . .

'Oh! thus,' quoth Dighton, 'lay the gentle babes:'
'Thus, thus,' quoth Forrest, 'girdling one another
Within their alabaster innocent arms:
Their lips were four red roses on a stalk,
Which in their summer beauty kiss'd each other.

        . . .

When Dighton thus told on: 'We smothered
The most replenished sweet work of nature,
That from the prime creation e'er she fram'd.'

        Act IV Sc iii

Richard has heard of another death – Anne's. He had her poisoned. Now he must marry Lady Elizabeth quickly – before Richmond does. The forces against him are growing; the Bishop of Ely has gone to join Richmond, and Buckingham has raised an army in Wales.

The curse bears fruit

Queen Margaret rejoices in Richard's plight. She hides when she sees Queen Elizabeth and the Duchess of York coming, weeping over the princes' death. Margaret approaches and reminds them how her husband and son were killed by the Yorkists. Now, of the House of York, the ones they loved are dead and only the wicked Richard lives. The three are united in their hatred of him.

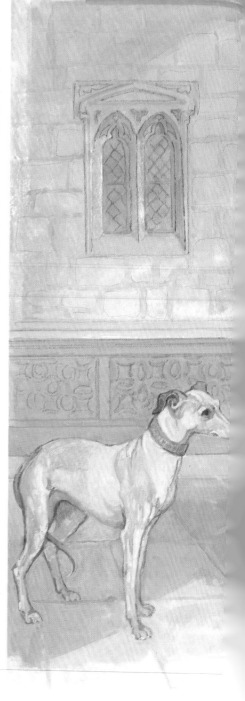

> **Revenge**
> *From forth the kennel of thy womb hath crept*
> *A hell-hound that doth hunt us all to death:*
> *That dog, that had his teeth before his eyes,*
> *To worry lambs, and lap their gentle blood,*
> *That foul defacer of God's handiwork,*
> *That excellent grand-tyrant of the earth,*
> *That reigns in galled eyes of weeping souls,*
> *Thy womb let loose, to chase us to our graves.*
> *O! upright, just, and true-disposing God,*
> *How do I thank thee that this carnal cur*
> *Preys on the issue of his mother's body,*
> *And makes her pew-fellow with others' moan.*
>
> Act IV Sc iv

Richard comes, looking for Elizabeth. All the women denounce him as a murderer. Then he asks Elizabeth for her daughter's hand. Scornfully she refuses; but he argues against her every objection. Finally she says she will consent – but she is lying.

Lords in arms

Richmond has landed with an army, and all over the country the lords are in revolt. Now Richard must fight for his throne. His forces capture Buckingham and lead him to execution. Buckingham remembers how Margaret warned him that Richard would be his death. Richmond, meanwhile, marches on, confident that God is on his side.

Richard's men pitch the royal tent at Bosworth Field, ready for battle next day. The other side do the same. They have a new recruit – Lord Stanley, who will join them secretly, although Richard holds his son hostage.

Richard and Richmond sleep in their tents. They are visited by ghosts in their dreams. One by one, Richard's victims appear; Henry VI and his son Edward; Clarence; Rivers, Grey and Vaughan; Hastings; Prince Edward and his brother; Anne; and last of all, Buckingham. Each curses Richard and wishes Richmond luck.

Ghostly voices
Let us be lead within thy bosom, Richard,
And weigh thee down to ruin, shame, and death!
Thy nephews' souls bid thee despair, and die!
[To Richmond]   Sleep, Richmond, sleep in peace, and wake in joy:
Good angels guard thee from the boar's annoy!
Live, and beget a happy race of kings!
Edward's unhappy sons do bid thee flourish.

Act v Sc iii

Next day both commanders address their men. Richmond tells his troops they are fighting a tyrant who has murdered his way to power. It is their duty to God to defeat him. Richard, shaken by his dream, makes an uninspiring speech. As he finishes, he hears that Stanley has taken his men to the other side.

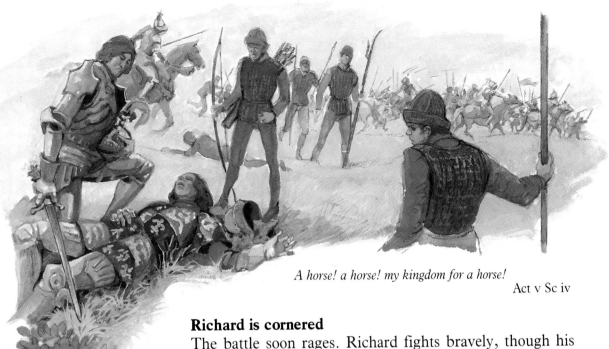

A horse! a horse! my kingdom for a horse!

Act v Sc iv

Richard is cornered
The battle soon rages. Richard fights bravely, though his horse is killed under him. He wants to kill Richmond in single combat. But when the two foes meet, Richard is slain. The victorious Richmond orders Richard's dead comrades to be decently buried. He intends to bring an end to the terror of civil war, where people kill members of their own families, for ever. He will marry Lady Elizabeth, and so unite the warring houses of Lancaster and York.

Peace returns
England hath long been mad, and scarr'd herself;
The brother blindly shed the brother's blood,
The father rashly slaughter'd his own son,
The son, compell'd, been butcher to the sire:

. . .

—God, if thy will be so,—
Enrich the time to come with smooth-fac'd peace,
With smiling plenty, and fair prosperous days!

Act v Sc iv

The play's characters

Richard

Richard's self-knowledge

And therefore, since I cannot prove a lover,
To entertain these fair well-spoken days,
I am determined to prove a villain,
And hate the idle pleasures of these days.

Act I Sc i

Richard

Shakespeare's original audience already knew what to expect when they first saw Richard III. In two earlier plays he had begun to murder his way to the throne. But in his portrayal of Richard in this play, Shakespeare had a surprise for them: a villain with a strong streak of humour, who can turn the sympathies of both audience and characters on to his side unexpectedly.

Richard proves himself an expert at manipulating people in the first act of the play. He uses Lady Anne's vanity against her, by insisting that it was love for her that made him the villain she already believes him to be. When he places himself in her power, by offering her his sword, she cannot believe he is not sincere. But he has calculated that she would not dare kill him – and he is right.

Throughout the play, Richard, like an actor, pretends to have a character that is the opposite of his true nature. He talks to the audience and takes

Anne

Anne's self-knowledge

Within so small a time, my woman's heart
Grossly grew captive to his honey words,
and prov'd the subject of mine own soul's curse

Act IV Sc i

them into his confidence, so that, sharing the joke, they come to see his enemies through his eyes, as fools who deserve what they get. Shakespeare also makes some of his actions sympathetic: Richard shows genuine courage at the end of the play, when he searches the battlefield for his enemy Richmond, and does not think of fleeing until the point of death.

Shakespeare balances this sympathetic portrait of his villain by showing how much the other characters hate and fear him, especially through their language. At various times he is called: 'Thou dreadful minister of Hell', 'Hedgehog', 'Thou cacodemon', 'Thou elvish-mouthed, abortive, rooting hog', 'That bottled spider', 'This poisonous bunch-backed toad', 'Hell's black intelligencer' and many other names.

Anne

Richard's queen is a victim of her own angry curse: when she agrees to marry him, she is so much under his spell that she forgets the dreadful fate she had wished upon his wife a short while earlier. She is never happy again: when we last see her, she is as terrified of him becoming king as Queen Elizabeth is. She is taken off unwillingly to be crowned, and dies by her husband's hand.

Richard

Edward

The princes

Edward and Richard are normal guileless children – fun-loving, intelligent and trusting. They enjoy a joke with their grandmother and their uncles. There is no malice in their mockery of Richard. They love and trust him, but they will not hear ill of their other uncles, and in their innocence suspect none in Richard.

Buckingham and Hastings

Lord Hastings is the sort of fawning but insincere man who follows those in power. He thinks he can outwit Richard, but Richard does not fully trust him. When Hastings' loyalty wavers, Richard is ready, and instantly turns against him.

Lord Buckingham is a better survivor than Hastings, more ruthless and willing to fall in with Richard's plans. But even he will go only so far; he will not co-operate in killing the young princes. Unlike Hastings, he realises when he has fallen from grace, and flees at once to the other side.

Buckingham

Buckingham's acting skills

Tut! I can counterfeit the deep tragedian
. . . ghastly looks
Are at my service, like enforced smiles;
And both are ready in their offices,
At any time, to grace my strategems.

Act III Sc v

Margaret

Duchess
of York

Elizabeth

Elizabeth baited by Richard

I had rather be a country servantmaid
Than a great queen, with this condition,
To be so baited, scorn'd, and stormed at:
Small joy have I in being England's queen.

Act I Sc iii

Elizabeth
Edward IV's queen is the one character who is almost a match for Richard at his own game. She became queen by winning the love of Edward, although she was a widow with grown-up children, and took care to see that her own family were given powerful positions at court. But after his death, she is almost helpless; Richard drives her to the sanctuary of the church, the last resort of the desperate. Even there, she fights back, bargaining with Richard over his plan to marry her daughter, while secretly supporting Richmond.

Margaret
Queen Margaret, in this play, is like a character out of a fairy-tale. She loathes all the other characters equally, curses them and foretells their fates like a bitter old witch. Her dark prophecies and angry retelling of their past crimes remind the audience that this story is part of a much longer history, and that Richard is not the only guilty one.

Duchess of York
The duchess is a kind, loving woman who deplores the fighting and killing in her family. Unusually for a mother, she sees her son Richard for what he is, and loathes and despises him.

Richmond
Henry Earl of Richmond appears suddenly towards the end of the play, untouched by the terrible past that Margaret keeps recounting. Though only distantly related to the dead King Henry VI, he is his heir, because so many others have been killed. To the other characters, he is a symbol of hope, and his final message of peace and reconciliation is the ideal of Shakespeare's time.

The life and plays of Shakespeare

Life of Shakespeare

1564 William Shakespeare born at Stratford-upon-Avon.

1582 Shakespeare marries Anne Hathaway, eight years his senior.

1583 Shakespeare's daughter, Susanna, is born.

1585 The twins, Hamnet and Judith, are born.

1587 Shakespeare goes to London.

1591-2 Shakespeare writes *The Comedy of Errors*. He is becoming well-known as an actor and writer.

1592 Theatres closed because of plague.

1593-4 Shakespeare writes *Titus Andronicus* and *The Taming of the Shrew*: he is member of the theatrical company, the Chamberlain's Men.

1594-5 Shakespeare writes *Romeo and Juliet*.

1595 Shakespeare writes *A Midsummer Night's Dream*.

1595-6 Shakespeare writes *Richard II*.

1596 Shakespeare's son, Hamnet, dies. He writes *King John* and *The Merchant of Venice*.

1597 Shakespeare buys New Place in Stratford.

1597-8 Shakespeare writes *Henry IV*.

1599 Shakespeare's theatre company opens the Globe Theatre.

1599-1600 Shakespeare writes *As You Like It*, *Henry V* and *Twelfth Night*.

1600-01 Shakespeare writes *Hamlet*.

1602-03 Shakespeare writes *All's Well That Ends Well*.

1603 Elizabeth I dies. James I becomes king. Theatres closed because of plague.

1603-04 Shakespeare writes *Othello*.

1605 Theatres closed because of plague.

1605-06 Shakespeare writes *Macbeth* and *King Lear*.

1606-07 Shakespeare writes *Antony and Cleopatra*.

1607 Susanna Shakespeare marries Dr John Hall. Theatres closed because of plague.

1608 Shakespeare's granddaughter, Elizabeth Hall, is born.

1609 *Sonnets* published. Theatres closed because of plague.

1610 Theatres closed because of plague. Shakespeare gives up his London lodgings and retires to Stratford.

1611-12 Shakespeare writes *The Tempest*.

1613 Globe Theatre burns to the ground during a performance of Henry VIII.

1616 Shakespeare dies on 23 April.

Shakespeare's plays

The Comedy of Errors
Love's Labour's Lost
Henry VI Part 2
Henry VI Part 3
Henry VI Part 1
Richard III
Titus Andronicus
The Taming of the Shrew
The Two Gentlemen of Verona
Romeo and Juliet
Richard II
A Midsummer Night's Dream
King John
The Merchant of Venice
Henry IV Part 1
Henry IV Part 2
Much Ado About Nothing
Henry V
Julius Caesar
As You Like It
Twelfth Night
Hamlet
The Merry Wives of Windsor
Troilus and Cressida
All's Well That Ends Well
Othello
Measure for Measure
King Lear
Macbeth
Antony and Cleopatra
Timon of Athens
Coriolanus
Pericles
Cymbeline
The Winter's Tale
The Tempest
Henry VIII

Index

Numerals in *italics* refer to picture captions.

Picture credits
p.3 National Portrait Gallery, p5 Birmingham City Museum & Art Gallery (photo Bridgeman Art Library). pp.6, 7, 8, 9 Geoffrey Wheeler, p.10 Royal Holloway and Bedford New College (photo Bridgeman Art Library).